BUBBLE BUBBLE

By Mercer Mayer

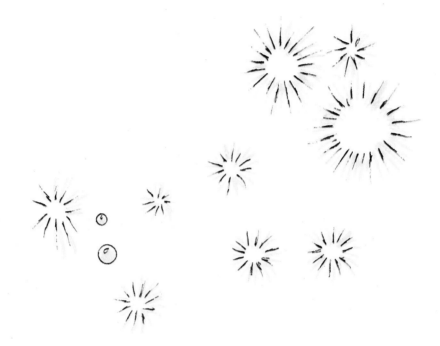

Packaged by John Sansevere

Library of Congress Catalog Card Number: 80-16777
ISBN: 1-879920-03-4
10 9 8 7 6 5

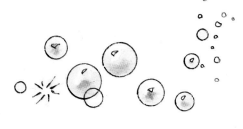

For Kenny Molles

One day as I was walking,

I bumped into a bubble.

It wasn't just one bubble, but lots of bubbles.

And they weren't just any kind of bubbles,

they were magic bubbles.

So I bought a magic bubble maker

and said good-bye.

I started blowing bubbles,

magic bubbles,

everywhere.

Then suddenly,

something strange happened!

Uh-oh, I thought.

I had to do something quick.

So I blew another bubble.

And that took care of that...

At least I thought so.

But I knew what to do.

I blew some more bubbles.

And that took care of that.

I wasn't worried one small bit.

I just blew another bubble.

And that took care of that.

I popped all the bubbles

one by one.

Blowing bubbles made me tired

so I went home.

Anyway, everyone knows there's

no such thing as magic bubbles.

MERCER MAYER was born in Little Rock, Arkansas, and grew up in Hawaii. He studied at the Honolulu Academy of Art and the Art Students League in New York City. He is the author-illustrator of many children's books, including *What Do You Do with a Kangaroo?*, winner of the Brooklyn Art Books for Children Citation; *Liza Lou and the Yeller Belly Swamp; The Wizard Comes to Town;* and *You're the Scaredy-Cat.* Among the many books he has illustrated are *Beauty and the Beast;* and *Everyone Knows What a Dragon Looks Like,* winner of the 1976 Irma Simonton Black Award and named one of the nine best illustrated children's books of the year by *The New York Times.* Mr. Mayer is also the creator of the best-selling Little Critter® series.

He and his wife Gina live and work together at their home in Roxbury, Connecticut.